Once Upon a Placemat
A Table Setting Tale

"Share a Meal, Not the Germs!"

Coloring book for cytomegalovirus (CMV) prevention

by

Lisa Saunders and Jackie Tortora

Interior illustrations by Marianne Greiner

ABOUT ONCE UPON A PLACEMAT

When Lisa can't remember how to set the table, her grandmother teaches her to listen to the silverware. How does Mr. Knife keep the dish from running away with the spoon? Why does Miss Cup insist she and the others get a bath before being shared?

Book includes recipes and germ prevention tips, especially against cytomegalovirus (CMV), the leading viral cause of birth defects.

Revised September 17, 2018

Books are available for ordering from your local bookstore, Amazon, Createspace, and my website, AuthorLisaSaunders.com, or by writing to me at LisaSaunders42@gmail.com.

REVIEWS

"Short story--big impact. *Once Upon a Placemat* finally accomplished what we could not--getting our kids to remember how to correctly set the table! Now, I hear my 12-year-old saying to herself, "Mr. Knife stands between Mrs. Spoon and Mr. Plate. Mr. Knife keeps his eyes and teeth toward Mr. Plate because he doesn't trust him since there was that time the 'dish ran away with the spoon.' What a brilliant extension to an old nursery rhyme. *Once Upon a Placemat* will also help your kids better understand the importance of washing their hands before meals and not sharing dishes before washing them first. Finally, a story that sticks!"
Dr. Rebecca Cihocki, Audiologist, Scottsdale, Arizona.

"A clever way to get across an important message about prevention of infectious diseases common to us all. Most people know how colds and flu are spread, but they don't know about how other germs are spread by sharing food, drinks and utensils."
Dr. Gail Demmler Harrison, Congenital CMV Disease Research Clinic & Registry

"The lesson of how to set a table is valuable as this is part of encouraging a family to sit down and eat together—a main intervention in preventing obesity."
Alison Dvorak, MS, RDN, CDN, Franklin, Connecticut.

"Lisa Saunders is always such an entertaining author. Her audience not only gets to enjoy a clever fairytale, but gets to learn important life lessons on how to protect babies from congenital CMV and other infections."
Marti Perhach, Group B Strep International

"I liked the simple storyline to help children remember tableware placement. The illustrations are adorable. Many of my friends are new grandmas—this is perfect for them to read to their grandchildren!"
Cindy Modzelewski, Richmond, Virginia.

DEDICATION

To the memory of Elizabeth Ann Saunders, whose mother, a licensed child care provider and the mother of a toddler, wasn't educated about CMV prevention until it was too late.

FOREWORD

Once Upon a Placemat is a charming story of how the eating utensils came to arrange themselves on the table in the time honored elegance of a table well set. In addition to creating an atmosphere for families to eat healthy dinners together, Lisa Saunders provides parents and caregivers with valuable information about how to prevent the spread of cytomegalovirus (CMV), the leading viral cause of developmental disabilities in infants. The information is easy to understand and yet very thorough. Great references for more information.

Dr. Joanne Z. Moore, Physical Therapist,
Certified Birth to 3 Early Intervention Provider
Joanne Z. Moore, PT, DHSc., is the owner of Shoreline Physical Therapy in East Lyme, Connecticut. She is the author of the guidebook, After the Loss of a Spouse: What's Next?

PREFACE

I first got the idea to publish "Once Upon a Placemat" as a stand-alone story when a friend texted me on Thanksgiving Day (2015) saying that when her niece MacKenzie was asked to set the table, she did so while telling the story of Mr. Knife and Mrs. Spoon, utensil characters from my children's novel, *Ride A Horse Not an Elevator.*

It occurred to me that my tableware characters could also be used to teach prevention of infectious diseases by reminding parents and children to never share dishes without washing them first.

My daughter Jackie came up with the title and book cover illustration for this fairytale in 1999 when she was 12 years old. She, too, had thought the tableware characters deserved a book of their own and created an additional adventure for them. Stay tuned for the next installment of this story to find out what happens next!

INTRODUCTION

Lisa Saunders in downtown Mystic, Connecticut. (Photograph by Meredith Fuller.)

Dear Parents, Grandparents and Caregivers:

Please enjoy this book with your children to teach them the correct way to set a table. This story is based on my relationship with my grandmother, expressed in my children's novel, *Ride a Horse Not an Elevator*. I include recipes from my grandmother's kitchen so you can enjoy the foods mentioned in this story.

I produced this book to inspire families to share meals without sharing germs. Miss Cup reminds us all never to share utensils, plates and drinks with anyone—especially pregnant women—and to be sure to wash our hands before setting the table or eating. I include more information for adults in my appendix about preventing congenital cytomegalovirus (CMV), the leading viral cause of birth defects—more widespread than Zika.

Please share this story with women of childbearing age because "Despite being the leading cause of mental retardation and disability in children, there are currently no national public awareness campaigns to educate expecting mothers about congenital CMV." (*Clinical Advisor*, June 21, 2014). I didn't know about CMV prevention until after my daughter Elizabeth was born with microcephaly.

I created a free downloadable program "kit" for parents, caregivers, and teachers to instruct children on table setting and germ prevention, particularly against diseases spread through saliva. It includes a coloring book of this story that can be downloaded as loose pages at no cost at: https://congenitalcmv.blogspot.com/2018/05/free-cmv-prevention-tool-kit-for.html. Or, the bound coloring book can be purchased on Amazon, CreateSpace or through me. There is also an edition of this book with the images colored in by Suzanne Doukas Niermeyer.

If you wish to arrange an author visit, write to me directly at LisaSaunders42@gmail.com.

Sincerely,

Lisa Saunders
Mystic, Connecticut
AuthorLisaSaunders.com
September 17, 2018

ONCE UPON
A PLACEMAT

Once upon a placemat, in Grandma's house not so far away, lived a plate, fork, knife, spoon, and cup. (*Can you see them peeking at you from behind the windows?*)

The tableware had many things to say, but I couldn't hear them until the day Grandma told me a story.

I loved to sit in Grandma's lap and listen to her stories.

I also loved to sit in Grandma's wheelbarrow and be pushed around her farm. In fact, I liked to sit and listen to stories all day long instead of helping with chores.

But one day, Grandma wouldn't let me sit. Grandma said, "Lisa, it's time for lunch. Please set the table."

"Grandma," I complained, "I never remember where all the silverware goes. Can't I just sit in the kitchen and watch you set the table while you tell me a story?"

Grandma agreed to tell a story as long as I helped.

First, Grandma made me wash my hands.

"If you don't wash your hands," Grandma warned, "naughty germs will try to sneak in your eyes, nose and mouth to make you sick!"

Once my hands were clean, Grandma got out her placemats and began to tell a story.

Grandma handed me a plate and said, "Mr. Plate loves to be the center of attention, so put him right in the middle of the placemat. He likes the utensils to gather around him so he can tell them stories about his favorite meals."

Next, Grandma took out the napkins.

Picking one up, she folded it in half. "You need to make a napkin look like a bed so Mr. Fork will get into it. He is very prickly and will only listen to Mr. Plate's stories if he's nestled in a nice, soft bed.

"Because Mr. Fork is a cranky fellow, put him on the left side of the plate. That way, he won't have to speak to the others—especially Miss Cup— who chatters way too much for his liking."

Grandma continued, "Now, put Mr. Knife and his wife, the shapely Mrs. Spoon, on the right side of Mr. Plate.

"You must be careful handling Mr. Knife because he's rough around the edges and can get very nasty when he feels he must protect Mrs. Spoon."

"Mr. Knife is particularly suspicious of Mr. Plate because he heard of the old nursery rhyme where 'the dish ran away with the spoon.'

"Put Mr. Knife with his sharp teeth toward Mr. Plate so he can bite him if he gets too friendly with his wife.

"Mrs. Spoon doesn't mind being separated from Mr. Plate because she is quite fond of Miss Cup, who sits right near her head."

Grandma explained, "Mrs. Spoon and Miss Cup are good friends because they can make chocolate milk together. And that makes them very happy!"

I giggled, because chocolate milk makes me happy, too!

Grandma continued: "With the exception of Mrs. Spoon, however, none of the others like Miss Cup.

"'Who does she think she is?' Mr. Knife often demands sharply.

"Mr. Knife is just jealous, because Miss Cup is the most popular of all the tableware."

"Miss Cup likes being popular with people, but she wishes they would give her a hot, soapy bath before sharing her. She gets upset when she hears people say to each other, 'I would like a taste of your drink—can I have a sip from your cup?'"

"Miss Cup often complains about this. She says, 'No one should share any of us without giving us a proper bath first—not even children with their mothers. Some people have germs that don't hurt them, but can hurt others—even unborn babies!'"

Grandma continued, "Miss Cup wishes people could hear her yell, 'I'm your drink—please don't share me!'"

"Grandma," I said, "I promise I will listen to Miss Cup and give her a bath before sharing her. I want her to be happy so she will make me chocolate milk!"

Finally, our table was all set and we sat down to eat.

Grandma served spaghetti and fruited gelatin for lunch. Miss Cup and Mrs. Spoon were so happy to be clean and next to each other they made me chocolate milk!

After lunch, I helped Grandma kill naughty germs by giving all the dishes a good bath. We dried them and put them away in their shelves and drawers.

I couldn't wait to set them out again for dinner. Grandma told me sweet Mrs. Fork was going to be invited because we were having cake for dessert!

Since Mr. Fork loves Mrs. Fork, even he will be happy!

And so will I!

Now that you've heard what your tableware is thinking, can you help set the table?

Remember:

- Wash your hands before you bring out the tableware.

- Mr. Plate is the star of every meal, so put him in the center.

- Mr. Fork is cranky because he's so prickly. He needs a napkin bed on the quiet side of the placemat, which is to the left of Mr. Plate.

- Mr. Knife is married to Mrs. Spoon. His teeth are toward Mr. Plate to keep him from running away with Mrs. Spoon.

- Miss Cup is near Mrs. Spoon's head so they can make chocolate milk!

Don't forget– never share your dishes with each other unless you give them a bath first!

DO YOU NEED HELP REMEMBERING YOUR LEFT FROM YOUR RIGHT WHEN SETTING THE TABLE?

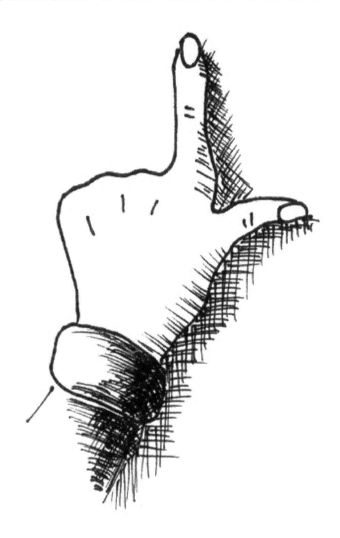

If so, try this:

Put your hands out in front of you, with only your thumbs and forefingers out. The hand that shows you the letter L, which is the first letter of the word 'left,' that is your left side.

Can you try this trick?

RECIPES OF "ONCE UPON A PLACEMAT" FOODS

Spaghetti

Cook spaghetti according to directions on box. Rinse spaghetti in cold water.

Spaghetti Sauce:
   1 onion
   1 green pepper
   1 clove of garlic
   1 pound ground hamburger meat
   2 cans (1 pound each) tomatoes
   2 small cans tomato paste
   Dash of Worcestershire sauce

Chop a small onion and green pepper and garlic. Cook in frying pan with one pound of hamburger meat. When meat is brown, drain the fat. Add 2 cans (1 pound each) tomatoes, 2 cans tomato paste and a dash of Worcestershire sauce.

Simmer meat sauce for 20 minutes. Mix in rinsed spaghetti and simmer for at least 1/2 hour, stirring now and then.

Note: When I was young, I liked to fork Grandma's spaghetti onto bread and make spaghetti sandwiches!

Fruited Gelatin

1 box gelatin dessert
1 to 2 cups drained canned fruit (my favorite was orange gelatin with canned fruit cocktail or pineapple)

Follow directions on gelatin box. Chill gelatin in refrigerator for approximately one hour. When the gelatin is slightly thickened, add the fruit and place in refrigerator until completely set (takes about 3 hours).

Chocolate Milk

In a large glass, mix:
8 oz. (1 cup) cold milk
2 ½ tablespoons chocolate syrup. Stir with Mrs. Spoon and enjoy!

Spice Cake

Preheat oven to 350 degrees. Grease and flour the cake pan.

Beat together:
1 cup sugar
½ cup shortening
1 egg
1 cup milk
2 tablespoons molasses
1 and 1/8 teaspoons cinnamon
1 teaspoon cloves*
2 teaspoons baking powder
1/2 teaspoon soda
2 cups flour

Grease and flour a 9 by 13 inch pan. Bake ingredients for about 20 minutes or until a toothpick comes out clean. When cooled, top with your favorite white icing or try cream cheese frosting.

*(Be careful: I accidently put 1 tablespoon of cloves instead of one teaspoon of cloves. Don't make that mistake!)

Note from Lisa Saunders: If you would like more stories about Grandma and me, plus several more recipes from her kitchen, read my book, *Ride a Horse Not an Elevator!*

"Once Upon a Placemat" is an excerpt from *Ride a Horse Not an Elevator*

A test of young courage. Lisa leaves the bullies and elevators of New York City to confront the outhouses, horses and eccentric relatives on her grandparents' farm. Accompanied by her loyal beagle, Donald Dog, Lisa faces a summer in a very different environment with its own challenges and dangers. Using an outhouse is the least of her problems! She is terrified of her new pony. When Lisa's grandfather is injured by a charging cow, he needs her to ride the pony to get help. Remembering Grandma's lesson about how love overcomes fear, she tries to push past her worries to get the help her grandfather needs. Book includes recipes from Grandma's kitchen, an author's study guide, and Cornell University's horse and human nutrition worksheets.

"A 'warm fuzzy' in paperback form. It is a tangible tale for storytelling that provides a springboard for discussion between children and adults."
Ruth Zwick, Educational Director, *Sentinel Publications*

'Ride a Horse Not an Elevator is a refreshing tale of a young city girl lucky enough to still have grandparents living on a farm. Using the horse as a magnet, we have tied Lisa's story of life's lessons in this child-friendly setting to agriculture, the care of horses and horse nutrition, to human nutrition and good eating habits, fitness and exercise."
Jeannie Griffiths, Cornell Cooperative Extension Horse Specialist, Department of Animal Science, Cornell University

APPENDIX

INFORMATION FOR ADULTS: DISEASES TRANSMITTED THROUGH SALIVA

by Lisa Saunders

Share a Meal--Not the Germs!

Table-Setting Fairytale Teaches How

Teachers/caregivers of young children are at greater risk for contracting diseases as are the children in their care: "Children cared for at daycare or in preschool education exhibit a two to three times greater risk of acquiring infections...**control measures are indispensable to the prevention and control of infectious diseases."** (Nesti et al, 2007).

Teach Infection Control!

Teachers/caregivers can share a meal with their students without sharing the germs! Teach the importance of handwashing and refraining from sharing cups, utensils and food.

Did you know there are many diseases spread through saliva? These include:

- Respiratory infections including influenza and croup.
- Strep throat, tonsillitis, and scarlet fever.
- Mononucleosis, commonly known as the "kissing disease," caused by the Epstein-Barr virus.
- Cold sores, caused by herpes simplex virus-1.
- Hand, foot, and mouth disease, caused by a strain of Coxsackie virus.
- Cavity-causing germs. "Babies are born without the bacteria that causes caries- the disease that leads to cavities. They get it from spit that is passed from their caregiver's mouth to their own. Caregivers pass on these germs by sharing saliva…" according to the American Academy of Pediatric Dentistry and Children's Dental Health Project.
- Cytomegalovirus (CMV). Congenital (meaning present at birth) CMV is the leading viral cause of birth defects. It causes developmental disabilities, liver disease, cerebral palsy and deafness as a result of infection in pregnant women. According to the Centers for Disease Control and Prevention (CDC): "People who care for or work closely with young children may be at greater risk of CMV infection than other people because CMV infection is common among young children..." (www.cdc.gov/cmv)
  - ➢ "Women at highest risk [for CMV] are those caring daily for children less than 24 months of age. These women, should they become pregnant, should either request to care for children over age 2 years for the duration of pregnancy or be tested for IgG antibodies to CMV. If they lack antibodies to CMV (immunity) they should care for children over age 2 years for the duration of pregnancy. If this is not possible they should carefully follow hygienic precautions and be retested for CMV monthly for the

first 5 months of pregnancy," states Stuart P. Adler M.D, Director, CMV Research Foundation.

How do you stop the spread of CMV?

According to the National CMV Foundation: (www.nationalcmv.org):

Do Not Share Food, Utensils, Drinks or Straws
Saliva may remain on food, cups or cutlery and could transfer a CMV infection to you and your unborn baby. Although it may be easier to feed your child from your own plate or you do not want to waste remaining food from your child's plate, it is best not to share food or cutlery.

Do Not Put a Pacifier in Your Mouth
How many of us are guilty of wanting to clean our child's pacifier by putting it in our mouth? Or, your hands are full and you put the pacifier in your mouth just to hold it for a moment? Saliva on your child's pacifier may transfer CMV to you and your unborn baby. Try to get in the habit of putting a pacifier on your pinky, not in your mouth.

Avoid Contact with Saliva when Kissing a Child
Try not to kiss a child under six years of age on the lips or cheek to avoid contact with saliva. Instead, kiss them on the forehead or top of the head and give them a big, long hug.

Do Not Share a Toothbrush
Toddlers love to imitate everything Mommy does, including pretending to brush their teeth with Mommy's toothbrush. Store your toothbrush in an area that your child cannot reach.

Wash Your Hands
Wash your hands often with soap and water for 15-20 seconds, especially after the following activities:
- Wiping a young child's nose or drool
- Changing diapers
- Feeding a young child
- Handling children's toys

How should you wash your hands?
According to the CDC (www.cdc.gov/handwashing):
- Wet your hands with clean, running water (warm or cold), turn off the tap, and apply soap.
- Lather your hands by rubbing them together with the soap. Be sure to lather the backs of your hands, between your fingers, and under your nails.
- Scrub your hands for at least 20 seconds. Need a timer? Hum the "Happy Birthday" song from beginning to end twice.
- Rinse your hands well under clean, running water.
- Dry your hands using a clean towel or air dry them.

ABOUT THE AUTHORS

Lisa Saunders

Lisa Saunders is pictured with Connecticut Governor Dannel Malloy while holding a photograph of her daughter, Elizabeth (1989-2006), at the ceremonial bill signing for Public Act 15-10: An Act Concerning Cytomegalovirus at the Office of the Governor in Hartford on July 28, 2015.

Lisa Saunders is a CMV education consultant, award-winning writer, and TV talk show host living in Mystic, Connecticut, with her husband, Jim. She is the author of more than 10 books and is a part-time history interpreter at Mystic Seaport. A former licensed day care provider, Lisa didn't learn about CMV prevention until after her daughter Elizabeth was born with microcephaly (small head/brain) in 1989. Elizabeth's story is told in Lisa's light-hearted memoir, *Anything But a Dog! The perfect pet for a girl with congenital CMV* (2008), translated into Japanese in 2017. She is the author of the 2017 article, "The Danger of Spreading CMV: How We Can Protect Our Children published by Child Care Aware® of America.

Lisa and her work helping Connecticut pass a CMV bill was featured in Cornell University's Alumni Magazine (Sept/Oct 2015) and widely covered in the media such as Fox CT and News 8. To educate entire families on CMV prevention in a fun and memorable way, Lisa published this short story, "Once Upon a Placemat: A Table Setting Tale," which includes a free teaching tool kit of a video and downloadable placemats for coloring.

www.authorlisasaunders.com

OTHER BOOKS BY LISA SAUNDERS

1. Help Childcare Providers Fight CMV(2018): A workbook for child care directors/policy makers.
2. Anything But a Dog! The perfect pet for a girl with CMV (Unlimited Publishing, 2008: The true story of a homeless old dog and the little girl who needed him. (Translated for Japan: Thousand Books, 2017)
3. Surviving Loss: The Woodcutter's Tale (2013): a tender fairytale for all ages about the process of healing after the death of a loved one. Inspired by the death of the author's daughter after a long illness.
4. Ride a Horse, Not an Elevator (2013): A chubby city girl leaves the elevators and bullies of her apartment complex for her grandparents' farm. Facing her fear of horses and outhouses, she finds a skinny friend who likes her just the way she is. Featured in Cornell University's "Horse Book in a Bucket" program.
5. Once Upon a Placemat: A Table Setting Tale (2016): When a young girl can't remember how to set the table, her grandmother teaches her to listen to the silverware. Will the dish really run away with the spoon? Book includes CMV prevention tips and lesson plan.
6. After the Loss of a Spouse: From Henry VIII to Julia Child (Act II Publications, LLC, 2016): Examines the bittersweet human condition of love and loss of 18 famous widow/ers including George Palmer Putnam (Amelia Earhart's widower), Mark Twain, C.S. Lewis, Martha Washington, Katharine Graham (of *The Washington Post*), Norman Rockwell, George Burns, Mary Todd Lincoln, Grandma Moses, Milton Hershey (Hershey's Kisses), Coretta Scott King, Captain von Trapp (of *The Sound of Music*), Hetty Green (world's greatest miser), William Gillette (aka Sherlock Holmes), Frances Wolfe Sisson (widow of Mystic, Connecticut, sea captain who perished in one of Texas's worst maritime disasters), and Abby Day Slocomb (widow behind Connecticut State flag design sent recently opened time capsule from Europe during WWI).
7. Mystic Seafarer's Trail: Secrets behind the 7 Wonders, Titanic's Shoes, Captain Sisson's Gold, and Amelia Earhart's Wedding (2012).
8. Ever True: A Union Private and His Wife (Heritage Books, 2004): True Civil War love letters reveal war's ever-present threat of death, scandals and infidelities. Includes the court-marshaling of a cow. Also a one-act "reader's theater".
9. Shays' Rebellion: The Hanging of Co-Leader Captain Henry Gale (2013): The dramatic events leading up to the noose around Gale's neck.
10. Mystic: Images of Modern America (Arcadia Publishing, 2016): The book of 164 images shows the evolution of Mystic, Connecticut, from a working-class village into a tourist driven community, while still embracing its quaint New England charm and keeping its rich history alive. Many of the images are in color and range from the year 1954 (Mystic's 300th birthday) through today. Co-authored with Kent & Meredith Fuller.
11. First Ranger Benjamin Church: Epic Poem About King Philip's War--Church Believed in Indians, God and Rum (2018): "I dedicated my poem to the memories of Native Americans who taught their ranger tactics to Benjamin Church, who in turn highlighted them in his memoir published in 1716. Soldiers trained in Native American fighting strategies have helped win wars throughout American history, including against Hitler's army in WWII." Book contains more than 40 contemporary photographs in New England that include Benjamin Church's sword, grave, and sites marking his haunts and homes during his life (1639 –1718). See images of locations for the Great Swamp Fight, mass grave at Smith's Garrison, Peas Field Fight, Church's capture of Anawan at "Anawan's Rock", where King Philip's head was mounted for 20 years in Plymouth and where King Philip's War began at Myles Garrison in Swansea, Massachusetts. Images related to Captain George Denison of Stonington, Connecticut, are included along with the approximate site of Canonchet's execution where he bravely declared, "I like it well. I shall die before my heart is soft, or I have said anything unworthy of myself."
12. Lisa's Guide for Writers (2013): Includes writing exercises and how to get published--even if you're not thin and famous!

Jackie Tortora

Jackie Tortora is a digital marketer living with her husband and children in upstate New York. Jackie created the title, "Once Upon a Placement" and additions to the tableware characters in 1999 when she was 12 years old.

ABOUT THE ILLUSTRATOR

Marianne Greiner is a freelance illustrator and teacher living in upstate New York.

SUGGESTED LESSON PLAN FOR CHILDREN

Staff can work it into STEAM (science, technology, engineering, art and math)*

Read aloud the fairytale, "Once Upon a Placemat: A Table-Setting Tale," then share a meal together. Help the children wash their hands and set their place setting by referring to the tableware characters. You can say things like, "Remember, Mr. Knife is afraid the dish will run away with the spoon, so put his teeth toward Mr. Plate" and "Miss Cup hates it when people share her without giving her a bath first because of those naughty germs."

If possible, give each child a "Share a Meal, Not the Germs" picnic kit with these suggested items:

- Bag (paper or reusable insulated bag).

- Plate, cup, napkin, fork, spoon, knife.
- Crayons or washable markers.
- Placemat with tableware characters (see last pages—good for laminating).
- Picnic food (homemade or prepackaged that would use all utensils, such as peanut butter, crackers, applesauce and cake).
- Hand sanitizer or sanitizing wipes.
- Sink hand-washing sign and tri-fold flyer on CMV prevention to take home (found on blog post: https://congenitalcmv.blogspot.com/2018/05/free-cmv-prevention-tool-kit-for.html)
- If funds are available, give a child their own bound copy of the coloring book version of "Once Upon a Placemat: A Table Setting Tale" to color and share with their families so their parents can reinforce the table-setting lesson and learn how to prevent CMV, the leading viral cause of birth defects virus, as well as other diseases.

*STEAM is a popular way to package and present the interconnectedness of Science, Technology, Engineering, Art and Math in the regular curriculum. When you talk about germs, the coloring book, "Once Upon a Placemat" (Art and Literacy), introduces germs (science, biology) in a format that integrates the arts. Drawing and writing activities can be planned to further integrate those domains. Teachers can further bring in technology and engineering by designing activities that help the children to "invent" equipment or machines to help better wash hands, keep food fresh and germ free, etc. Math can enter into the plan by graphing how long children wash their hands, how often they wash their hands, how many uses the classrooms get out of a single pump bottle of hand soap, etc. With a little more thought (and a few trips to Pinterest!), lots of germ-based activities can be created and integrated.

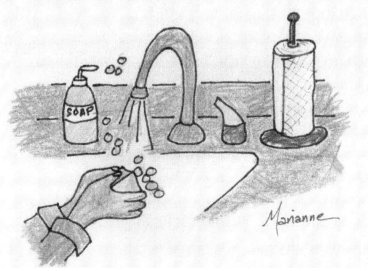

Once Upon a Placemat: A Table-Setting Tale

(just the words if you that is what you need for a lesson plan).

Once upon a placemat, in Grandma's house not so far away, lived a plate, fork, knife, spoon, and cup. The tableware had many things to say, but I couldn't hear them until the day Grandma told me a story.

I loved to sit in Grandma's lap and listen to her stories. I also loved to sit in Grandma's wheelbarrow and be pushed around her farm. In fact, I liked to sit and listen to stories all day long instead of helping with chores. But one day, Grandma wouldn't let me sit. Grandma said, "Lisa, it's time for lunch. Please set the table."

"Grandma," I complained, "I never remember where all the silverware goes. Can't I just sit in the kitchen and watch you set the table while you tell me a story?"

Grandma agreed to tell a story as long as I helped. First, Grandma made me wash my hands. "If you don't wash your hands," Grandma warned, "naughty germs will try to sneak in your eyes, nose and mouth to make you sick!" Once my hands were clean, Grandma set out her placemats and began to tell a story.

After she handed me a plate, she began, "Mr. Plate loves to be the center of attention, so put him right in the middle of the placemat. He likes the utensils to gather around him so he can tell them stories about his favorite meals." Next, Grandma took out the napkins. Picking one up, she folded it in half. "You need to make a napkin look like a bed so Mr. Fork will get into it. He is very prickly and will only listen to Mr. Plate's stories if he's nestled in a nice, soft bed. Because Mr. Fork is a cranky fellow, put him on the left side of the plate. That way, he won't have to speak to the others—especially Miss Cup—who chatters way too much for his liking."

Grandma continued, "Now, put Mr. Knife and his wife, the shapely Mrs. Spoon, on the right side of Mr. Plate. You must be careful handling Mr. Knife because he's rough around the edges and can get very nasty when he feels he must protect Mrs. Spoon. Mr. Knife is especially suspicious of Mr. Plate because he heard of an old nursery rhyme where 'the dish ran away with the spoon.' So, put Mr. Knife with his sharp teeth toward Mr. Plate so he can bite him if he gets too friendly with his wife. Mrs. Spoon doesn't mind being separated from Mr. Plate because she is quite fond of Miss Cup, who sits right near her head. Mrs. Spoon and Miss Cup are good friends because they can make chocolate milk together. And that makes them very happy!"

I giggled, because chocolate milk makes me happy, too!

Grandma continued: "With the exception of Mrs. Spoon, however, none of the others like Miss Cup. 'Who does she think she is?' Mr. Knife often demands sharply. Mr. Knife is just jealous, because Miss Cup is the most popular of all the tableware. Miss Cup likes being popular with people, but she wishes they would give her a hot, soapy bath before sharing her. She gets upset when she hears people say to each other, 'I would like to taste your drink—can I have a sip from your cup?' Miss Cup often complains about this. She says, 'No one should share any of us without giving us a proper bath first—not even children with their mothers. Some people have germs that don't hurt them, but can hurt others—like unborn babies!' Miss Cup wishes people could hear her yell, 'I'm your drink—please don't share me!', but no one can," sighed Grandma.

"Grandma," I said, "I promise I will listen to Miss Cup and give her a bath before sharing her. I want her to be happy so she will make me chocolate milk!"

Our table was finally set so we sat down to eat. Grandma served spaghetti and fruited gelatin for lunch. Miss Cup and Mrs. Spoon were so happy to be clean and next to each other that they made me chocolate milk! After lunch, I helped Grandma kill naughty germs by giving all the dishes a good bath. We dried them and put them away in their shelves and drawers. I couldn't wait to set them out again for dinner. Grandma told me sweet Mrs. Fork was going to be invited because we were having cake for dessert. Since Mr. Fork loves Mrs. Fork, even he will be happy. And so will I!

Now that you've heard what your tableware is thinking, can you help set the table?

DIAPER WIPES DON'T KILL CMV!

(CMV is #1 Birth Defects Virus)

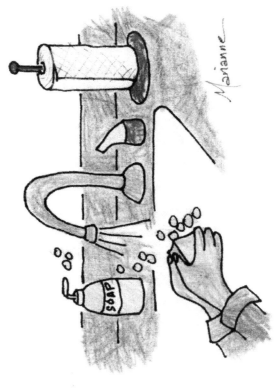

Some infections hurt unborn children. Always wash your hands after touching bodily fluids and never share cups and utensils—especially with toddlers who may be excreting cytomegalovirus (CMV). Diaper wipes don't kill CMV! If soap and water are not available, use an alcohol-based hand sanitizer that contains at least 60% alcohol (but still wash with soap and water as soon as possible). Learn more to protect unborn children at: CDC.gov/CMV

Reference: "Cytomegalovirus Survival and Transferability and the Effectiveness of Common Hand-Washing Agents against Cytomegalovirus on Live Human Hands" (Stowella et al., 2014). Sign produced by Lisa Saunders, author of "Once Upon a Placemat: A Table Setting Tale" and "Help Childcare Providers Fight CMV." Illustrated by Marianne Greiner. Colored by Suzanne Doukas Niermeyer. Want to color in your own signs and books? Visit the "Child Care Providers Fighting CMV Project" at: CongenitalCMV.blogspot.com

"Once Upon a Placemat"

Dear Parents, Grandparents and Caregivers:

Please enjoy this placemat and my book, "Once Upon a Placemat: A Table Setting Tale," with your children to teach the correct way of setting a table in a fun and memorable way. You can also use "Once Upon a Placemat" as a tool to prevent the spread of infections transmitted by saliva by reminding children never to share utensils, plates and cups with anyone—not even family members—and to be sure to wash their hands before setting the table or eating! Lisa Saunders, author and parent representative of the Congenital Cytomegalovirus Foundation: congenitalcmv.org

Did you know there are many diseases spread through saliva? These include:

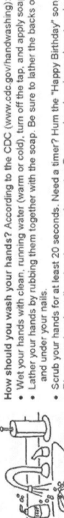

- Respiratory infections including influenza and croup.
- Strep throat, tonsillitis, and scarlet fever.
- Mononucleosis, commonly known as the "kissing disease," caused by the Epstein-Barr virus.
- Cold sores, caused by herpes simplex virus-1.
- Hand, foot, and mouth disease, caused by a strain of Coxsackie virus.
- The #1 viral cause of birth defects, congenital (meaning present at birth) cytomegalovirus (CMV)—the most common cause of nonhereditary sensorineural hearing loss in childhood. Congenital CMV can also cause developmental disabilities. According to the CDC, congenital CMV causes one child to become disabled every hour in the U.S.

How can you protect your unborn baby from congenital CMV? The risk of getting CMV through casual contact is small—it is generally passed to others through direct contact with body fluids, such as urine and saliva. CMV is often being shed by apparently healthy toddlers. Therefore:

- Avoid putting your child's food, utensils, drinking cups, and pacifiers in your mouth.
- Kiss your children on the forehead or cheek instead of the lips.
- Wash your hands after changing diapers, wiping runny noses, picking up toys. (More: cdc.gov/features/prenatalinfections)

How should you wash your hands? According to the CDC (www.cdc.gov/handwashing):

- Wet your hands with clean, running water (warm or cold), turn off the tap, and apply soap.
- Lather your hands by rubbing them together with the soap. Be sure to lather the backs of your hands, between your fingers, and under your nails.
- Scrub your hands for at least 20 seconds. Need a timer? Hum the "Happy Birthday" song from beginning to end twice.
- Rinse your hands well under clean, running water. Dry your hands using a clean towel or air dry them.

If soap and running water are not available, use alcohol-based hand gel.

When a young girl can't remember how to set the table, her grandmother tells her a story. Read "Once Upon a Placemat: A Table Setting Tale" to learn why the knife keeps a sharp eye on the plate and why the cup insists she and the others get a bath before being shared. Book includes germ prevention tips and a placemat image for coloring. Fairytale written by Lisa Saunders & Jackie Tortora; illustrated by Marianne Greiner. Order book in shops, Amazon or AuthorLisaSaunders.com. For author visits, or to order larger printed placemats in bulk, contact: LisaSaunders42@gmail.com. Share your colored placemats--take a photo of it and upload to: facebook.com/onceuponaplacemat.

Made in the USA
Middletown, DE
09 January 2020